Nene's Prose II

Ancel Mondia

Ukiyoto Publishing

All global publishing rights are held by

Ukiyoto Publishing

Published in 2023

Content Copyright © Ancel Mondia

ISBN 9789360163709

*All rights reserved.
No part of this publication may be reproduced, transmitted, or stored in a retrieval system, in any form by any means, electronic, mechanical, photocopying, recording or otherwise, without the prior permission of the publisher.*

The moral rights of the authors have been asserted.

This is a work of fiction. Names, characters, businesses, places, events, locales, and incidents are either the products of the author's imagination or used in a fictitious manner. Any resemblance to actual persons, living or dead, or actual events is purely coincidental.

This book is sold subject to the condition that it shall not by way of trade or otherwise, be lent, resold, hired out or otherwise circulated, without the publisher's prior consent, in any form of binding or cover other than that in which it is published.

www.ukiyoto.com

Contents

Twenty-eight (October 12, 2022)	1
Hustle (November 18, 2022)	5
Viva Magenta (December 30, 2022)	9
Self-talk (February 13, 2023)	12
Pendulum Clock (April 14, 2023)	16
Analyzing A Video (June 23, 2023)	21
About the Author	24

Twenty-eight (October 12, 2022)

The ninth month its second day has dawned on me. I am gratefully turning twenty-eight in spirit and body. While some people are ashamed of their real ages, I take pride in declaring that I am gracefully aging.

I am having double chin, flabby arms, and uneven skin tone as signs that my youth is gradually fading. As I obviously noticed the physical changes in me, I initially felt ugly and insecure. However, when I stared long at my own reflection, I slowly began to see a beautiful person.

I had been soaked in the warm and uplifting sun, and in the cool and comforting rain. I had stepped on the sandy and stony shores of wisdom, and on the grassy and dusty fields of courage. My profound and diverse experiences are the apparent and permanent beauty of my existence.

Turning twenty-eight indeed is a veritable milestone, which I happily celebrate and sincerely thank for. My past years are never a waste because each of them has meaningfully contributed to this very moment.

They have carved my heart, molded my mind, and written my soul. My birthday has become indescribably special and uniquely significant to me as I have constantly acquired multiple insights in this lifetime.

Wildest dream in unexpected time

I had been criticized and ridiculed for my inclination to poetry. My love for creativity had been mistaken for love for immaturity. People insisted that my poetic side was a mere childishness, which I should change about myself. Nevertheless, I consistently declined to fully surrender my wildest dream of becoming a published poet.

A year ago, I humbly started to administer my own Facebook Page, Tula ni Nene, where I occasionally post my literary pieces. It was beyond my expectation that it was already the making of my poetry, which later on was traditionally and digitally published. I officially authored published books in my twenties, and it overwhelmingly brought me personal fulfillment.

Honor weighs more than popularity

I sometimes got tapped to compose literary pieces to be performed by participants in local contests. I wholeheartedly did my part without even thinking about the chance of winning or risk of losing. There was a time when my contender championed and I, remaining in the background, felt genuinely happy for the team.

Last year, I passionately wrote a Hiligaynon poem termed as binalaybay, for the performance of a contestant. The group sadly failed to secure a place in the literary competition.

However, among all the pieces presented, it was only my poem that was being praised by a principled writer in town. I knew I should stick to the honor of art and not give in to popular systems.

Support from circles of strangers

Due to lack of motivation at times, I was taking irregular pauses to actively update the content of my social media. I frequently thought that nobody was really checking on my timeline or waiting for notification from me. Nevertheless, I surprisingly found myself wrong when an unknown subscriber dropped a supportive comment.

I felt alive and driven everytime my followers left positive and uplifting feedback. They made me realize that genuine support could come from random people despite the fact that I had only connected with them online. I knew I was appreciated and loved for the efforts I exerted to openly share my literary gifts with various people from different walks of life.

I am fully conscious of the reality that every upside has a downside. I can become an unaware object of somebody's frustrating envy. I can become an intended victim of somebody's wicked disrespect. I can become an unintentional nemesis of somebody's threatened superiority.

But if there is one single thing I can assure anyone, it is that all I try to do toward others is guided and determined by goodwill. My kind stance shall strongly remain true as I have turned twenty-eight and for more years to come.

Hustle
(November 18, 2022)

Every time I scroll through my social media feed, a polysemous word keeps on surfacing: hustle. I was intrigued, so I googled the word that had been linked to the concepts of haste and force.

I was unsure of the meaning, so I researched the usage of the word in today's context. I came to comprehend that "to hustle" had been defined as "to work tirelessly". I initially thought that I had been slothful since I had never considered myself overly sober about work.

Then the internet introduced me to the notion of "hustle culture" which had been also known as "burnout culture". I then realized that I should not feel guilty for staying relaxed or being calm while working. Making ends meet or earning a living should not be about overwork or exhaustion.

I had come from different employers, and my work experiences with them taught me to take the idea of hustle in a different light. My own definition of HUSTLE indicated the crucial things, as I believe, that should be considered in the working life: Health, Usefulness, Success, Truth, Living, and Existence.

Health

As I was hired as a contract employee in a cooperative, I knew that the work environment should promote and support well-being. Performing clerical work or undertaking routine duties, without consideration to overall health would frustrate and derange us. We should hustle to keep ourselves driven and sane, not otherwise.

Usefulness

When I was employed as a registrar in a high school, I deeply understood that the work system should encourage the utilization of brains and skills. Holding a rank, which was merely visible in the organizational chart, would stagnate and degrade us. We should hustle to make use of our qualifications and strengths, not let them fall into disuse.

Success

As I was hired as an editor in a newspaper, I instantly realized that the work relationships should fuel the appetite for accomplishments. Treating others as a negative competition, which commonly happens between offices, would limit and fail us. We should hustle to materialize collective success, not obstruct or disable it.

Truth

When I was employed as an online teacher in a learning center, I profoundly comprehended that the work rules should consider the employees' perspectives. Exaggerating the customers' rightness, with disregard to the personnel's knowledge and values, would complicate and invalidate us. We should hustle to live our acquired truth, not to disown and compromise it.

Living

As I was hired as a writer in a digital company, I immediately sensed that the work demands should help and improve the workers' lifestyle. Creating work-life imbalance, which had been a method of exploitation, would drain and kill us. We should hustle to better or upgrade the quality of our lives, not to be manipulated and deprived of life.

Existence

When I was employed as a coordinator in a tutorial business, I greatly understood that the work plans should stress the practicality of the vision. Setting ideals and goals, with a lack of realistic and solid foundation, would fool and waste us. We should hustle to experience our own coming to existence, not just for the sake of existence.

I have been through many work experiences that put me in a never-ending transition. I have always known that I would keep on evolving as all have been fluid and none were set in stone.

In the spinning and stirring world, where words are constantly changing contexts and definitions, it would be within our power to contextualize and redefine the word 'hustle.'

Viva Magenta (December 30, 2022)

Very Peri (PANTONE 17-3938), the color of 2022, signifies empowering newness. It has no doubt played a huge influence in my transformative year.

In 2022, my Filipino poetry book, Tula ni Nene, marks my debut as a published author. My two poem collections, Nene's Poetry and Ikalawang Koleksyon, and one prose compilation, Nene's Prose, follow in the same year. I deem the year 2022, characterized by Very Peri, as a wish fulfillment, a dream come true, and an answered prayer.

I have thought that my literary achievement is the endpoint of my existence, but I have proven my long-standing belief utterly wrong when I remain substantially alive as the new year is steadily approaching.

I have patiently waited for the much-anticipated announcement of the color for 2023, and the trending news on Viva Magenta (PANTONE 18-750) has absolutely satisfied my senses and preferences.

From Beginning to Breakthrough

As Viva Magenta is a fearless color that represents self-expression and strong wit, I know I shall be wholly grateful and blessed when I finally receive my trophy for an award from my publisher, Ukiyoto.

In October, I surprisingly opened my inbox containing a congratulatory email. The message stated that I made it to the Ukiyoto Literary Awards 2022-23 and was selected as an awardee in the category, Fiction - Woman Writer of the Year, for my title, Nene's Prose.

I believe I am still at the beginning of my writing career, but the literary recognition already signals my pending breakthrough. As my acknowledged prose is a compilation of my personal essays, I shall welcome 2023 with an intimately joyous celebration.

From Potential to Profession

Since Viva Magenta is an audacious color that mirrors assertive spirit and sheer fortitude, I expect I shall be profoundly existent when I eventually broaden my horizons by landing a new occupation.

By the end of 2022, I declined to renew my employment contract. As I made the pivotal decision, I again found myself in relief and happiness. A few interested employers already reached out and interviewed me as their prospective employee.

I realize having power over myself means empowering my potential and being true and open to my desired profession.

From Worst to Win

While Viva Magenta is an unconventional color that depicts healing grace and empathic strength, I suppose I shall be manifestly authentic when I essentially appraise my connections and relationships in general.

Before the 31st day of December, I thoughtfully resolved to wisely manage my personal life, that includes my family and friends. I opted to prioritize sustaining my peace of mind over being on good terms with everyone that I certainly would never be at peace with.

I fully expect that the worst has to happen between me and others before I can remove blockages that potentially deprive me of my deserved win in life. As I have grown into a 28-year-old lady, I shall embrace 2023 with protective and life-giving love.

My New Year's resolution is to convert a beginning to a breakthrough, a potential to a profession, and a worst to a win. With God's and the universe's graces, I shall be my own story and version of Viva Magenta.

Self-talk
(February 13, 2023)

I was a child who knew what I wanted in life, but my mind was led astray as I was growing up. I lost the dream, I lost myself. But now I am awakened, and realize that I shouldn't trade my inner child for anybody or anything else.

I have come to this point in my life without even asking for others' consent. But I did it. And no one can stop me. I now have the wings and nobody can break them. I will break free from the cage where I dwelt for too long. Nobody can pass on their issues, fears, and mediocrity to me.

I have tried to be respectful, but if respect is being used as oppression and manipulation, I better respect myself more than I am able to respect others. I am the one who will choose my battles and I resolve to go with the flow of change. I won't surrender to any forms of blockage.

I won't plant myself in a place where I'm not meant to be rooted. I'll hold on to my prayers. Nothing can bring me down. I'll follow my own advice, I'll follow my own star. Because I know better.

No one can say that my decision is right or wrong. I'll always gain and lose something at once, so I'll choose what I want. Whatever the consequences will be, I am the one who'll face them. So I'll decide for my life where there's no one else to blame.

I am my own person. I am not the vicious cycle they have tried to eternalize. I am not the destructive pattern they tried to perpetuate. I am here to put a stop to the cycle. I am here to put an end to the pattern. I am here to be my own person.

I won't try to fit the ideals or reach the standards of others. I am my own ideals and standards, being in the era when everyone has the right and choice to follow their star. I am created to evolve and integrate to unite with the universe.

Don't anybody dare entrap me in their primitive thoughts. Don't anybody dare negate me by their groundless judgments.

Change is the only phenomenon that is constant and permanent. For change to be in favor of me, I'll transform that change into evolution and integration by being a never-ending process.

Not everyone will cheer for me. Not everyone will find me deserving of greatness and triumph. But I'll do my thing. Enhance my skills. Unleash my passion. Despite the setbacks and doubts being thrown at me.

People will always question me, criticize me. But I won't live just to prove them wrong or impress them.

People that live in shame, choose to be in shame. So they wish to drag me with them. Trying to mislead me into thinking that I'm not enough, that I don't deserve greatness and triumph that only the universe can offer.

These people aren't the ones who'll guide me. I can never share fulfillment with them. They are astray, and it's nonsense to let myself be directed by them. They don't know the face of greatness and triumph, which I am meant to be. They only know the face of shame and regret, which they have always been. They are blockages.

I have the choice to remove the programming or conditioning done to me. I'll speak against the injustices they have inflicted on me and stand against the oppression they have imposed on me.

I may feel alone, but I know I'm not. The universe backs me up, my spirit guides accompany me, the Supreme Being watches over me. They will unfold the best destiny for me when I attract and manifest the right things.

I won't participate in negative competitions that are ruled by envy. I won't be in a rush to win compliments that are never real, never pure. These people will always see me as a threat and a rival.

They will only poison my mind to live in shallow ways. They will only corrupt my heart to live in a superficial manner. They will only turn me into anybody like them. So I won't be tricked, I won't be fooled.

When my actions and thoughts are determined by their reactions and words, I'm already in a critical condition. But I'll pray to God. Instantly. Constantly. Only the Supreme Being can save me.

It's better to feel alone than to be wickedly accompanied. I'll be my higher self and eventually my soul tribe will find me.

Pendulum Clock
(April 14, 2023)

Despite the randomness of my experiences throughout my life, the pendulum clock maintains its rhythmic and swinging activity. Its hands eternalize the circular motion, and its pendulum perpetuates the back-and-forth movement.

At this juncture of my life, I have realized the connection of the pendulum clock to my human existence.

Last year, I resigned from my job as I refused to renew my contract. I knew I would be in a lose-lose situation if I chose to stay. The circumstances became unfavorable and discouraging to me.

I worked more than I was paid, my salary only served as my allowance so I could man the office. I couldn't see an opportunity of getting absorbed or regularized, despite being the right hand and pioneer in the office.

I dealt with various difficult personalities, strict office hours, and daily traffic congestion. I could only take so much so I left my job without remorse. I made a leap of faith because all I ever wanted at that time was to break free from my situation.

During my job hunt that seemed to have become a hiatus, the symbolism of the pendulum clock became profound and personal to me, as I associated it with my concept of sacrifices, boundaries, and rejections.

As a symbol of sacrifice

As days and nights passed me by, like the predictable circular motion of the hands in the clock, I grew impatient and hopeless about finding a new job.

I even contacted my friends through messenger for the sake of killing time and inquiring about available job offers. It appeared to me that I had an ill-timed resignation since I remained unemployed for months.

I also got offended when one of my pals texted me that I should sacrifice before I could succeed. I tried to control myself from overthinking about what she actually meant, but I came to think that she assumed that I had an easy-breezy life.

I knew I had been struggling in the background and how to be me had been a roller coaster. My past achievements were the fruits of my labor, I worked smart for my hard-earned successes.

As the pendulum moved to and fro, I had been through sacrifices and successes as paired experiences. I succeeded because I sacrificed.

I didn't need to hold a public viewing for my sacrifices to prove that I had them. They were unseen but never the reason to consider them nonexistent or to invalidate the successes they actually produced.

As a symbol of boundaries

I grew easily irritated and overly sensitive during my waiting period, particularly when the people close to me pressured and hurried me to find a job again. They gave me unsolicited advice that I didn't find helpful in any way.

I realized that I was quite exhausted from running around in circles for long, similar to the second hand of the pendulum clock. I believed and obeyed them, but I found my years wasted and saw myself straying.

They told me to go offline, stay silent while online, or refrain from posting, so an employer would have an interest in me and hire me. But I let their advice go in one ear and out the other because I knew I wouldn't want that kind of employer anyway.

I believed my online self wasn't supposed to be treated as my working self. I post on the internet without mentioning my employment affiliations, and I knew it would be pointless for me to subdue my online self.

As the pendulum moved from side to side, I believed there should be boundaries between work identity and online identity. They shouldn't be treated as one, they were both aspects of life and neither could be the entire identity.

As a symbol of rejection

There were people who wanted me to pursue the career path that they thought would be the most beneficial to me. But I silenced them by listening to myself this time, as I searched for job offers based on my preferences.

Although I got rejected multiple times, I didn't stop the search. I came to realize that I had difficulty during my job hunt because my previous experiences weren't aligned with what I had been passionate about.

But I reached the point in my life where I became willing to make things feel right for me. I prayed that there would be an employer that would be willing to give me the chance.

As the hands of the clock repeatedly completed their cycle, I repeatedly searched for job offers, passed my resume, and got informed of the rejection. But I bounced back like the pendulum that effortlessly moved back and forth.

I realized that rejections were actually redirections. If I wasn't meant for the left side, I would move to the right side, and vice versa. And finally, I was given the chance by an employer.

The pendulum clock indeed is a metaphor for my life on earth. It has the circular motion and the back-and-forth movement that has been visible in my human experiences.

It is inevitable that my own pendulum clock shall stop in the far future, but when it does, I shall always want to have it stop in peace, joy, and love.

Analyzing A Video (June 23, 2023)

I happened to watch a video that talked about femininity. It received different reactions and contradictory comments. Some netizens agreed and some argued. In my case, I watched the video a few times before I was able to compose this reaction post.

My initial thought about the video's message is that it was conflicting.

The first viewpoint presented there was that women should embrace their feminine essence. I oppose this idea since our biological qualities do not always equate with our energies. We have male and female as sexes, and masculine and feminine as energies. But male and masculine are not one, as female and feminine also are not one.

I am female, but it doesn't mean that all I have or should have is feminine energy. Despite my gender, I have both the masculine and feminine energies. This is why we have the concept of balance and integration. We need to balance our energies within in order to integrate ourselves because we are naturally made up of both masculinity and femininity.

Falsifying an energy in us makes us imbalanced and unnatural, so we become self-destructive instead of self-sustaining. So the first viewpoint from the video, in my perspective, is fallacious.

The second viewpoint presented was that society changed the idea of femininity so women focused on their appearances instead of being true in their heart. I have come to think that the cause of the problem is the concept of being true in our heart. We have been misled by the belief that a woman is or should be utterly feminine.

We are women, and we have both the masculine and feminine energies, individually and naturally. So being true to our heart means having the balanced energies of masculinity and femininity within us. Embracing the so-called feminine essence is a delusion since biological quality as a determinant of energy is nonexistent.

What makes us focus on our appearances instead of our truth starts from the idea that our physical attributes should determine our energies. Society imposes this false thinking, and sad to say, the speaker in the video was programmed by this society which he thought he stood against.

This condition makes the video's message more conflicting since the speaker's argument has holes that make his second viewpoint vague and shaky.

The third viewpoint presented there was the analogy of women attracting men to honeys attracting bees. This reminds me of the concept of gender bias that women should attract and men should chase. It goes back to the notion of feminine and masculine energies that causes me to emphasize that whether a body is female or male, it is both feminine and masculine.

We are more than gender roles, we are individuals of both femininity and masculinity. It is our own individual choices whether we attract or chase a particular person, thing, or circumstance, since we are the ones who can figure out the effective way to have what we want.

We should not be restricted or permitted by the biased concept of appearances and energies, our actions should be determined by our truth. With this analysis, I find that even the third viewpoint from the video is too far from the truth.

About the Author

Ancel Mondia

Ancel Mondia was awarded Fiction - Woman Writer of the Year by Ukiyoto Publishing in 2023.

www.ingramcontent.com/pod-product-compliance
Lightning Source LLC
LaVergne TN
LVHW041602070526
838199LV00046B/2101